SHADOW
of
DANGER

BETTY JEAN CLARK

SHADOW *of* DANGER

BETTY JEAN CLARK

SHADOW
of
DANGER

ARPress
45 Dan Road Suite 5
Canton MA 02021

Hotline: 1(888) 821-0229
Fax: 1(508) 545-7580

Ordering Information:
Quantity sales. Special discounts are available on quantity purchases by corporations, associations, and others. For details, contact the publisher at the address above.

Printed in the United States of America.

ISBN-13:   Paperback   979-8-89389-709-8
                  eBook   979-8-89389-789-0

Susan Miller is a registered nurse who works at Lexington Hospital in Lexington, South Carolina. She works in a nursery, where she is responsible for the care of newborns. She adores her job and looks forward to going to work every day. It might be challenging at times because babies are frequently born addicted to drugs. Up until the time of their birth, their mothers were drug addicts. These babies require extra attention and love. They wail all day and, on rare occasions, all night. Susan is heartbroken for these innocent babies and prays that God would intervene. These babies have already had a difficult life and feel helpless.

Susan's shift was done. She told the girls she'd be going back home. A shadow sprang from nowhere behind her, when she got into her car. She started hurrying as a result. As she reached the door handle, she felt a man smacking a handkerchief on her face. When she woke up, she had a tremendous headache. Her stomach felt uneasy too, as though it rolled. She was all hot, sweaty, and puzzled. Susan tried to figure out where she was and thought she wouldn't puke if she shut her eyes and laid still. She remained motionless and fell asleep.

She still had a headache the following time she woke up. As she looked around, she noticed a filthy foul odor room. She looked down at where she was laying and raised her elbows slightly, she noticed the mattress she was lying on, it's completely stained, and there's no sheet, blanket, or pillow.

"How could somebody be that filthy dirty?"

Just being here made her feel filthy. Susan prays and cries, pleading with God to assist her. *"Please Lord Give Me Strength. Help to move my legs. I have to get out of this place."*

Susan though about her job, where are her purse, and car keys? She has no way to call anyone. She couldn't contact anyone because she didn't have a phone. Ok Susan focus, think, and figure it out. Dangle your legs and get the feeling back in your body. She does and she slides down to the floor. She begins to move but felt dizzy. She understands she must regain her strength. Someone in the hall is approaching and unlock the door. It was the man with ski mask on and a hoodie. He has something in his hand. And he must be crippled. He walks with a shuffle to his legs. As the man approaches her, she runs out the door, attempting to figure out how to get out of the two-story house. Susan runs but fails as her feet still not working right but she gets up and down the stairs she goes taking every other step. And finally, she discovers a way out, but the man was just behind her so she rans real fast as she knows her life depends on her getting away as quickly as possible.

When he realized he wouldn't be able to catch her, he released the vicious dog and it sounded like a killer dog. She was terrified and out of breath from running so hard, but she had to keep it. She got her foot in a vine while running, which tripped her, fell head-first over a steep bank, rolling and rolling till she fell all the way down. However, the dog came to a complete stop right there. She gets up and runs away quickly and continue to run. Susan began to notice that it was getting late, and she was starving. She must think about getting close to the highway. While going about and listening to the sounds, she heard something. Finally, the closer she goes to the sound, the clearer it becomes that it is a major highway. She dashed to the source of the obnoxious noise. How fortunate is she? But she came to a fence. A barbwire is fastened to it. She is extremely cautious while climbing down the other side and she lands in a ditch.

Susan got out of the ditch and a man reaches out to her with his hand. She was too terrified because this man could be him as she never got the change to see his face. She couldn't turn around and go back. So she grabs his hand and he lifts her up.

"Hello, my name is Henry Cole," he says.

Susan introduced herself by saying, "Hello Mr. Cole, my name is Susan Miller."

"When I saw you going up that barbwire fence, I thought to myself, "This girl is fleeing something." Am I correct?" Mr. Cole asked.

"Yes, I was kidnapped and drugged at an old farmhouse. There's a man who appears to be crippled, as if he had polio or something. He is the owner of a vicious dog. He grabbed me and took me away from my job." Susan stated.

"Where is your job?" he asked.

"I work as a registered nurse in Lexington, SC, at Lexington Hospital. "I look after newborn babies in the nursery," She informed Henry of what had occurred. "I wanted to speak with a cop and tell him what had happened to me."

"I agree, and I'll contact the Sheriff, but first, I'll need to find out where you live."

"I live in a condo in the Common Gardens in Lexington, South Carolina. I have my address written down." Susan said "yes."

"Okay, I'll call the Sheriff and tell him what you told me; he'll want to speak with you." he said.

So Mr. Cole called the Sheriff and was told that he would be there in a few minutes and to keep Susan at the truck stop until he arrived. "Now I'm going to call my wife, Dot," So he loaded Susan into his truck and called his wife, telling her everything Susan had told him. Dot told her to bring her in and said, "I'll get the room upstairs ready." "Okay, we are on our way."

He told Susan that they have a large truck stop just up the road.

"Wow, you and your wife?"

"Yes,"

"You are right, it is big," Susan said as they pulled in, "and we love it, Susan."

Dot was waiting for them. She met them and was attempting to persuade Susan to join her. She figured Susan Miller was scared. "Oh my Lord, what a terrible thing for you to have gone through," Dot exclaimed. "I am so sorry you had to endure such a terrible experience."

"Thank you, Mr. Cole." Says Susan.

He said, "You are very welcome. Now go along with Dot." So she went ahead and did it.

"I'll show you around," Dot told Susan. "This is my store; it offers everything, and I also have a restaurant, which is managed by Bessie. You'll meet her tomorrow. I'll get you something to eat and a place to sleep right now." So she got Susan some turkey & ham with cheese and the trimmings and a coke and chips and they went upstairs. Dot showed her the shower, and she advised her to wait until she saw the Sheriff before showering. "OK," Susan said.

"This man kidnapped you for a reason, Susan, and the Sheriff, Sam Lucas, is a fine sheriff, and he'll figure it out. You're fortunate that my husband arrived when he did. God alone knows how long you'll be wandering around." Dot stated.

Susan remarked, "You two must be angels."

"That's something I'm not sure of." I'm sure Henry and I have helped a lot of people, and we both enjoyed it. Susan, we have a twin bed here, and I just changed the linens, and the shower has everything you'll need. And there's a dead bolt on this upstairs door that leads to the basement. Nobody knows you're here, so you're safe," Dot said "Here comes the Sheriff now. He will be right up, and I will go down to meet him."

"All right, Miss Smith, my name is Sheriff Sam Lucas, and here is Anna, one of my deputies. We want to talk about what happened to you. Would you mind telling me your full name and where do you go to work, by the way? The sheriff started asking questions.

"Susan Ann Miller is my name, and I work at Lexington Hospital in Lexington, South Carolina and I live in a Common Gardens condo in Lexington, South Carolina. I am a registered nurse who works in a nursery with newborn babies." Susan responded.

"What is the address of your apartment? Do you have a cell phone?" The sheriff immediately investigated.

"Well, it was stolen." Susan replied.

"Do you recall the phone number?" "Yes," and she informed him of the phone number.

Do you have a car? Can you tell us the make and model and its color? The sheriff asked.

"Yes, it is 201 9 Buick La Saber, with a white exterior and a grey inside." Susan replied.

"Where do you park your car at work?" The Sheriff followed up with a question.

"In the back of the hospital grounds," Susan answered.

"Thank you. Susan, please tell us what happened to you.

"Okay, I was at work at the hospital and my shift was over. I went to my car. While I was walking, I saw a shadow coming up behind me. As I placed my hand on the handle, a man's hand slapped me on the face with a cloth and down I went to the concrete. When I woke up, I could not remember where I was and how I got there. I have got a bad headache and my stomach feels like rolling. I was dizzy and broke out into a cold sweat. "I told myself to close my eyes and lie down so I wouldn't vomit, but the next time I woke up, I still had a bad headache but felt better, though I was still not sure where I was," Susan recalled the incident. "I realized I needed some strength to break out and escape from a filthy spot when I heard a large dog barking furiously. I lifted myself up with my elbows and saw the filthy mattress I was lying on, and I couldn't believe I was still on it. I dangled my legs from the bed and let them fall.

Susan continues to narrate, "Once I got moving, I felt dizzy and off-balance, but I was determined not to get back on that mattress." I briefly halted. "I was formulating a plan for an escape. When I heard someone approach, he unlocked the bedroom door. He was clad in a hoodie, with a ski mask over his face. He shuffled as he moved, therefore he must have been physically disabled. I rushed to the door, leapt out, and began searching for an exit. I quickly made my way downstairs and out the door. He tried to grab me from behind. I slipped out of his grasp. I kept on running. He knew he had lost me, so he unhooked the large dog. And, while I was sprinting rapidly, I slipped on a vine and tumbled down a very steep slope. Until the very end, I continued rolling until the large dog didn't came after me. He halted on a steep slope. I got up and kept sprinting. Running all day left me exhausted and starving. It was getting late, so I walked slowly. So I looked around."

"Susan, that must have been quite an experience for you. I'm sorry for what you had to go through. You are a strong woman," Sheriff's remark. "Would you be willing to visit our local hospital for tests? Anna will drive you there and stay with you and, afterwards, she will bring you back to the Truck Stop. You are safe. I swear." Susan agreed to go.

Anna is awaiting her return and, on the way, back to the truck stop, she asked Susan a few things, "Are you in a relationship, Susan?"

"I was in a relationship three months ago that ended when I found out he was dating another girl." Susan explained.

Anna responded, "Could you tell me a bit about him? I'm curious as to where he lives. What does he do for a living? Do you happen to know what his phone number is?"

"Yes, I can give you all that information, but why do you need it?" Susan asked.

"We like to have every piece of information as a lead while investigating a crime. Because they role play, we don't always get to know a person on the inside." Anna clarified. Susan nodded and handed him the piece of paper on which she had written his ex-phone boyfriend's number and address.

Susan was told by Anna to get some rest and to call her if she remembered anything else. Anna accompanied her into the Truck Stop, where Dot greeted them. After what had occurred to Susan, Dot felt really bad for her. Dot gave Susan some food "Here are some Turkey breast and ham sub with chips. What would you like to drink?"

"Well, I am really thirsty." Susan said.

"So, would you like some Coke and perhaps some tea or coffee later?" Offered-Dot.

"Absolutely." Susan replied.

"Sure, I'll go up with you because I have your phone. I took the liberty to provide you a nightgown and slippers; they are on the bed." Dot remarked.

Susan said, "Thank you; I was just thinking what I was going to do with the clothes."

"There are nightgowns and slippers available, and I can get you some pants and tops for tomorrow, as well as anything else you need. Also, here is the phone and a phone card for now until you can get yourself a better one soon." Dot noted.

"OK," Susan said, "I'm so amazed by you. You have been a lifeline for me. I was so worried about my clothes and my phone. I have been concerned about my job and my bank account too. OK, the issues have been resolved. Thanks again. See you tomorrow."

After eating, Susan took a shower and cleansed her hair. She had a good feeling about herself. She took the phone and the phone card, added the minutes, and then called Dot and Henry to give them her number. So they'll be able to contact her if they need to. She slept and had dreams and, at 5:00 a.m., she awoke. She took a shower before making a list of things she needed to do. Because the places didn't open until 9:00 a.m., she couldn't make any calls. So she was grateful for Dot's gift of a notepad and pens. When she contacted her job at 7:00 a.m., she stated, "Susan, the sheriff from over there, had already called me and gave me all the details of what happened to you." I've put you on paid medical leave. You can come in whenever you're ready, and we'll take you off medical leave. When you're ready, your work will be waiting for you."

"Thank you," Susan said. Susan hung up and dialed her bank's number. The teller informed her that her account had been frozen, that someone had repeatedly entered the incorrect password, and that her card had been barred. "Your money is still in your account, but since you don't have the card with you and can't come in… We'll cancel this card and send you a new one. Your money will go on the new card. However, it will have to go to your home because we have your address from when you initially signed up here. Can you get someone to pick up your mail in 7 days?

Susan thought about having Anna pick up her mail and say goodbye to the teller.

Dot told Susan and said that Henry is going to put a buzzer on her door. "Security will be set up today in that room. We are setting it up today. If anyone wants to come in and climb the stairs, it will be on tape."

"Good," Susan said to Dot, "I'm going down to get something else to eat."

"Come on down, and I'll introduce you to Bessie, who runs the restaurant, she will make you some breakfast." She took her to the restaurant and introduced to Bessie, "Bessie, I want you to meet Susan Miller, can you make her something for breakfast? And Bessie, it is on the house, she is our guest."

"Sure Susan," Bessie responds to Susan's request and begins to prepare bacon and eggs, wheat toast, and coffee. While Susan waited, she called Anna and asked if she could have pick up her mail in 7 days because the bank is sending her a new debit card." Anna agreed to pick her card in 7 days.

Susan got her food, and Bessie remarked to her, "I'm truly sorry for everything that has happened to you. They told me in secret and warned me not to tell anyone else. I promise I won't. I hope you have a good time with the food." Susan ate her food while Bessie went back to work today.

Susan headed up to the bar once she finished her meal. "I saw you glancing over your shoulder, and I'm wondering if you're worried he'll come here," Bessie said as she noticed Susan peering over her shoulder.

Susan remarked, "Yes, but I had no idea what he looked like. He wore a ski mask and a hoodie. I had no idea what kind of vehicle he drove. All I know is that he walks like he is crippled. Well, that may be enough."

"Susan, I think we may have arrested your kidnapper," Mr. Cole stated as he dialed Susan's number. He's been brought into custody by the Sheriff to be questioned. He wants me to dial your number."

"The man got out of the truck and began questioning us about the girl. He had a photograph of you, and it was you who was in it. We all answered no, and we have very few women coming here. Usually, they are with a boyfriend or husband. I called the Sheriff and informed him of the situation. He dashed for his truck as soon as he noticed the Sheriff. However, he was apprehended by the Sheriff." Mr. Cole said.

He came to a complete halt in his truck.

"Sir, put a muzzler on the dog," the Sheriff instructed. The man was apprehensive about doing so. The Sheriff then instructed once more to put a muzzler on the dog. So he did." The man was told to take small steps down by the Sheriff.

"What for officer, what did I do wrong?" the man responded.

"First, you make an attempt to escape." "Then you started refusing to put a muzzle on that vicious dog, which made you suspicious of me," she says.

The dog warden arrived and took the dog away, while the man was arrested. He appeared to be crippled.

An hour later the Sheriff came to see Susan. "Your test came back, and you may not want to hear this," he warned.

"Yes I do. I want to know everything. Susan was ecstatic.

"You were, after all, raped multiple times. We linked some fiber with certain hair follicles. Mack is his given name. It was a perfect match. Today is the day he will find out everything. First and foremost, I wanted to inform you. We've got our man, Susan. We also have another individual on our hands. Do you know who the second man is? Your ex-boyfriend is the second man." "What? What role does he play?" asked Susan, "We interrogated him. And he was jittery, and he explained that he was working on his family tree. We happened to see your name while he was showing it to us. So he'd shifted the conversation away from your surname being on his family tree. We informed him that we intended to question you. He made an attempt to refuse. We warned him, if he refused to go, we'll be able to know if his hiding something. So, he set out. He also attempted to take the laptop. And we told them he couldn't bring it and that should stay here. We detained him and interrogated him. We proceeded to his residence and conducted a search of his place and invited Ed to visit. He's a computer programmer. He had discovered the truth. Your ex-boyfriend wasn't researching his family tree. He was tracing yours. One of your old bibles was discovered in his belongings when he moved out of your flat. There was a complete list of the family's names, addresses, and birthdays inside the bible. Ed discovered that you had a great aunt that your family never knew because your grandfather never mentioned. Your great aunt was a wealthy lady. Some of information was discovered as a result of our inquiries. Your great grandfather may be so old, but he was still able to tell us what we needed to know. So, instead of working on his own family tree, he was working on yours. And after discovering this information, he decided to pay Mack to kidnap you. They'll keep you in custody until you receive your inheritance, and then I'm afraid they'll kill you. Susan, you must not leave your room on the second floor. Henry will be with us." The Sheriff stated, "You'll know who's there when you hear the buzzard. If the person is a stranger You are not going to let them in. Okay, whatever you want to say. We will also offer you with a television so that you do not become bored. You can also learn about any changes by monitoring the news every day. We're rather certain there are others engaged so always stay in the room and make sure you know who you let in. Your stairwell door will be secured with a deadbolt. I'll take you up the stairwell now. In 6 days, Anna will go fetch your mail. I bought you a notepad and pens, and I'll bring you a television. You also have my business card. You can reach me or Anna at any moment. I'll be seeing Mack and your ex-boyfriend." He then vanished. He must have spoken with Henry and Dot because security arrived and installed a monitor, a new lock on the door, and a buzzard. Her meals were delivered right to her front door.

Susan was visited by Deputy Anna after a week had passed. She inquired as to how she was doing and whether she was able to sleep at night. Susan answered that she has been experiencing flashbacks of the man and the dog. Aside from that, she's OK. "This bag here has your mail," Anna explained, "and there are clothes in this bag. I will pick up some other things too like your laptop, hair dryer, and curling iron, makeup in case you need them, and I got some a notebook, pens, and a couple of books. I'm going to go fetch those items from the car", Susan began sorting through her mail, and one letter in particular caught her attention. Susan let Anna in as she was returning from her cruiser. She examined the letter before handing it over to Anna. There was no forwarding address included in the package. "Let me open it," Anna said. ***WE ARE LOOKING FOR YOU, WE WILL FIND YOU***, it said as she read. Just some crooked letters in Colored pencil and the picture of a rope with a hangman drawing on it.

Anna informed Susan that she needed to report this letter to the Sheriff. This implies that the first two are linked to someone else. "You're fine, we have security in place, Susan. As well as a deadbolt it will be caught on video if someone comes up here. Are you all OK, Susan? This is what we all do as women," She presented her with a pepper spray canister.

"You spray it directly to their faces. Keep it with you at all times." She bid Anna farewell and stood there watching her walk away. She then called Social Security and requested a a new social security card. She then called DVM and informed them that she had misplaced her driver's license, and that they would be providing her a replacement. She then reported the stolen identity to the Federal Trade Commission. She was then told to dial a few more numbers. She can buy a replacement phone for $125.00 and all of her information on the other lost phone will be blocked, which she did.

Mr. Cole had called him and claimed there was still another man looking for you, the Sheriff told Susan Miller, "He informed me that he had a photograph of you and that he was showing it to everybody. The men were stalling while they looked at it. So he could dial my number. I drew up alongside him as he started the car. He then jumped into his car and began driving away. I had requested assistance. He took off, and I told him to come to a halt. He continued on, although he didn't get very far. He was surrounded by officers and eventually came to a halt. We put him in handcuffs and took him inside. He'd turned in his phone along with the rest of his belongings. And everything was on his phone. On the inside of his billfold was paper with everyone's names, as well as the addition and subtraction of what each person's cut would be. In his truck, he had paperwork detailing who gets a piece of the money. We also discovered who the other players are. Susan, it's all right. I informed you. I'll get back to you as soon as possible." Susan checked her mail once more and activated her debit card. and proceeded to read the rest of her mail. She thought to herself, "Wow." Is it possible to solve this issue and give her the freedom to go wherever she wants? She wishes that these men receive everything that is due to them.

Susan answered yes when Bessie called and asked if she could come up. When she spotted Bessie approaching from the monitor, she opened the door and welcomed her in. "There's a special on the news tonight," Bessie Smith told Susan. I was hoping we'd be able to watch it together. Susan did, after all, turn it on. The Sheriff was summoned. "Ladies and gentlemen," he said, "Sheriff Sam Lucas is my name, and I'd like to speak with you. A young lady was kidnapped, drugged, and raped multiple times about 15 days ago. She is a nurse, and she was on her way home from work. A man rushed up behind her and slapped a towel over her face as she reached for the door handle. It was drenched in narcotics. She then collapsed. She didn't wake up for several days, and this man continued to inject her with drugs. Would you do it if the girl was your daughter? Would you keep your evidence a secret or would you reveal it? This young lady worked as a registered nurse. She was dedicated to her career and worked hard at it. She never failed to show up for any of her appointments. She was not deserving of such treatment. You should come forward if there are other people engaged in this case. Because these men are imprisoned. Offer a suggestion for plea bargaining They're also willing to talk. They are well aware that the deck is stacked against them. There will be no plea bargaining if they don't tell the entire store. And believe me when I say that they want to plead guilty. So, if there's anyone else involved, they'd better step up right now. We'll come after you if these folks start talking. There are phone numbers at the bottom of the screen if you have any questions. Thank you all so much."

"What a great guy he is. I'd cast my vote for him. He works for the people. Anna, Deputy Anna is nice too. She has been quite helpful to me." Susan made her thoughts known.

"Yes, Susan, they are. They help me, so did Mr. and Mrs. Cole." Replied Bessie.

"What went wrong with you? Or perhaps it isn't my place to ask." Asked Susan.

"Yes, Susan, I'd like to share it with you. A mad man was following, and he would not leave me alone. As I was approaching to my car, I notice him holding a butcher knife, I reached into my pocket and sprayed him in the face with pepper spray. He took off running and I immediately drive straight to the police station and report the incident," Bessie continues, "Every day, no matter where I was, he would emerge, and so I kept running," Bessie adds.

"What a dreadful thing, Bessie. When did this happen to you?" Susan asked.

"It was around ten years ago. The Cole's also helped me. I also put bars on the windows, the downstairs, and the basement. Then I made the entire house more secure. I feel safe." Bessie answered.

"Yes, and I do as well. They also added security in this area." Susan agrees.

Bessie hugged Susan Miller and said, "this will be over before you know it."

"I've liked your company. Bessie, I was surprised when you told me about your life." Susan said.

"Well, I don't tell just anyone… but I wanted you to know that I understand how you feel. I was terrified of this man, and I desperately wanted it to be safe." Bessie remarked.

"Bessie, I appreciate you sharing this. I don't feel so alone anymore." Susan was grateful for her help.

Susan thanked Sheriff Lucas straight away for speaking up on her behalf in the news about what she had been through.

"You're more than welcome. The reason I phoned you is to inquire about your family."

So, she informed him about herself and her family, including where they all resided. Although I am an only child, I have a large family. Then he told her what he'd discovered. "The man who kidnapped you has begun to speak. He is aware of the test results and is aware of the evidence stacked against him. He's aware he won't be able to get off. However, he is not the leader. Your ex-boyfriend is the leader. He hired the group. He is the one responsible for the whole thing. The kidnapper confessed and everyone else involved in the crime," The Sheriff continued to explain everything to Susan, "… you might get a better night's sleep tonight. I also gave your phone number to the proprietor; Mr. Johnson is his name, and he wants to see you, so he'll phone you and set up an appointment for 9:00 a.m. tomorrow. Mr. Cole has told me that if you wish, he can take you to his office. He said he wouldn't mind, and we have all of your possessions, including your phone, handbag, vehicle, and keys. Your car had been towed; it is currently parked at the Truck Stop. It has been thoroughly examined to ensure that there is nothing wrong."

"How can I ever thank you, Sheriff?" Susan feeling deeply grateful.

He stated that this is a unique situation and that he will keep in touch with her soon.

The next day, Mr. Johnson called her at and asked if he could see her at 9:00 in the morning in his office if she could make it and responded she would be there. So, she called Mr. Cole and he said yes, he would be happy to take her, "so can you let me know when you are ready? And I will come down."

"Yes, I can." Susan got ready and he was waiting for her. It was the first time in weeks that she had been out of her room. Mr. Johnson was waiting to see her when they got there. After offering her hand, she asked Mr. Johnson if Mr. Cole could join them. And Johnson was quick to respond with "as you wish."

She learns she has an inheritance when Mr. Johnson informs her of it. "Your great aunt Mary, who's seen you grow up since you were young," is something he told her about. "…you don't know her, but she's willing to give you her home and property anyway. I will assist you with your life management. Your proposal contains a large number of stocks and bonds. She'd done it all in your name long before she died. She was a smart lady, and she was extremely wealthy. You won't have to work, ever. She took credit card applications set up under your personal bank account registered in your name. The is well managed with servants. I will let you know when you can take control of your inheritance. Please try to be patient. I have to have you sign all this paperwork, then it will be filed, and taxes will have to be paid. I promise you it won't take too long till you can move in. Also, we will have some movers to help you move in."

Another month went by, and Susan went to court for the trial of the five men involved in the kidnapping, drugging, and rape of her. All five men admitted their guilt. They were all sentenced and were taken back to their cells. Susan believed that justice had been done in her case.

Mr. and Mrs. Cole had to go get some boxes to help her pack her belongings at her apartment so she could move in. Susan's landlord stated that she will miss. She shared the news that she was moving with all her friends but tight-lipped about the specifics of the inheritance. Mrs. Cole emptied and cleaned out her refrigerator and Mr. Cole went to the store and brought back the essential things that Susan would need to stay in her apartment. Susan, like Mrs. Cole, was filled with emotion and cried.

Now she has her car back. Mrs. Cole drove Susan's car and Mr. Cole brought his truck. He unloaded her things that she had out of his truck. So she could pack. Mrs. Cole held Susan in her arms and told her to call her every day so she would know she was okay. She said, "We never had kids, but you make me feel like we do now. I have grown fond of you."

Mr. Cole came in and he came over to them and he put his arms around them, and he agreed with Mrs. Cole. "Okay, Susan, we must depart; we love you as if you were our own. Be patient with Mr. Johnson. He will call you soon." And they left.

THE END